FOLLOW YOU HOME

SIDEKICK

to the novel

by

ELIZABETH HALPRIN

Published by

WeLoveNovels

Disclaimer: This publication is an unofficial Sidekick to *Follow You Home* and does not contain the novel. It is designed for fiction enthusiasts who are reading the novel, or have just finished. Order a copy of the novel *Follow You Home* on Amazon.

WeLoveNovels maintains an independent voice in delivering critical analysis and commentary; we are not affiliated with or endorsed by the publisher or author of *Follow You Home*.

Questions? Ideas? Comments?

Email founders@welovenovels.com.

We are listening!

Table of Contents

INTRODUCTION	7
EXPLORING THE AUTHOR'S FICTIONAL WORLD	11
CHAPTER ANALYSIS & DISCUSSION	13
CHARACTER GUIDE	31
A CLOSER LOOK:	33
THE UNRELIABLE NARRATOR	37
IMAGINING ALTERNATE ENDINGS	39
THEMES & SYMBOLS YOU MAY HAVE MISSED	43
POSSIBLE STORYLINES FOR A PREQUEL	47
HIDDEN CLUES	49
IN THE FINAL ANALYSIS . . .	51
IF YOU LOVED THIS NOVEL . . .	53
ABOUT THE AUTHOR OF THIS SIDEKICK	56

Follow You Home
A Sidekick to the Mark Edwards Novel

Introduction

Mark Edwards's *Follow You Home* is about everything you always knew was lurking in the shadows. Every time you were walking home alone and heard something behind you. All the monsters that lived under your childhood bed. And all the worst stories you heard on the news and thought, "but that can't happen to me!"

Daniel and Laura are an ordinary couple whose biggest concerns are whether or not they'll have kids and if they'll be too homesick to enjoy Stockholm. They get on an overnight train from Budapest, Hungary, to Sighisoara, Romania, worn out from two months of travel. They befriend a Romanian couple and share a few beers. And then the night begins to spiral out of control.

When they get back to their home in London, everything is different. They're behaving oddly, and their colleagues and friends don't recognize them. What happened after they got on that train in Budapest will turn their lives upside down, but they'll keep it a secret for better or worse.

Children are told the story of Hansel and Gretel for a reason: to teach them to stay away from dark woods and the dark houses inside such woods. It's too bad these childhood lessons don't always stick.

The author and co-author of several chart-topping novels, Mark Edwards's latest work, *Follow You Home,* is a bestseller in both the United Kingdom and the United States. Edwards likes to write about scary things happening to regular folk, and *Follow You Home* is no exception.

How to Get the Most out of This Sidekick

The next two sections of this Sidekick—*Exploring the Author's Fictional World* and *Chapter Analysis & Discussion*—will be most useful while you are reading the novel. You can also refer to the *Character Guide* for a quick "who's who." All subsequent sections—from *A Closer Look* all the way

Follow You Home
A Sidekick to the Mark Edwards Novel

through to *If You Loved This Novel*—are designed to be read <u>after</u> you have finished the novel.

Wherever you are in your reading of the book, with this Sidekick you'll get a chance to dive a little deeper into the author's world, spend some more time with your favorite characters, and check out some of the book's themes and symbolism. There might even be a few Easter eggs along the way.

If you don't have a copy of *Follow You Home* yet, be sure to pick one up before you get started—after all, here be spoilers! (Don't worry, they're clearly marked.) You can order a copy of the novel on Amazon.

* * *

Disclaimer: I'm not Mark Edwards. I don't know Mark Edwards. Neither I nor WeLoveNovels has any association with Mark Edwards whatsoever. What you've got in your hands is 100% independent and unauthorized opinion, commentary, and analysis.

Follow You Home
A Sidekick to the Mark Edwards Novel

Follow You Home
A Sidekick to the Mark Edwards Novel

Exploring the Author's Fictional World

*F*ollow *You Home* is set in two primary locations: London, England, and Romania. Though Romania is now a prosperous country, in the imagination of Western Europe, it's still associated with Soviet communism and vampires—thanks to Bram Stoker's *Dracula*. In this novel, as seen through the eyes of a young British couple, Romania is a shadowy and mysterious place. Though living in Europe, Romania's Slavic and residual Ottoman influences make the nation seem very foreign to Daniel and Laura. In contrast, their hometown London is a bustling big city leagues away from the lush forests that populate Romania. The two places contrast sharply in terms of modernity, at least as far as they are depicted by Edwards—it seems possible that magic and monsters may actually exist in the forests of Romania.

In the afterword, Edwards describes a situation in which he and his girlfriend had to hitchhike across France after losing their passports. Though nothing too horrible happened to them, the English news outlets were reporting all sorts of crimes against English citizens abroad, which he ascribes to "British paranoia." There certainly is a flavor of that paranoia in Edwards's narrative, the well-to-do traveler's fear of unpredictable foreign lands based upon shallow understandings of economic development, poverty, and crime.

Follow You Home
A Sidekick to the Mark Edwards Novel

Chapter Analysis & Discussion

Part One: Hungary–Romania August 2013, Chapters 1–8

The opening scene of a dark train platform immediately puts us on edge, suggesting every figure that emerges from the shadows is dangerous. None of these suspicious characters, however, becomes a villain; what happens to Daniel and Laura is all the more terrifying because it's just bad luck. They had the rest of their vacation (and their lives) planned—a few missteps send them careening off that path and into disaster. Their illusion of control and safety is afforded by wealth, nationality, and modern technology, but all of that is easily taken away. The vulnerability of life to chance, and the ease with which the wonderful can become awful, is much more frightening than some creep on a train.

Daniel and Laura's journey after being thrown from the train is a composite of nightmarish archetypes, from their lost identities to the feral dogs, the woods, and of course, the house. Daniel keeps willing the night to become day, wishing for clear sight and rationality to return. Human fear always fills darkness with horrors, but it seems this time that the horrors are all too real.

The house, surrounded by dead foliage, sets off Daniel's "lizard brain." Something awful is in that house that humans have been hard-wired to avoid: some primitive, ancient evil from which, perhaps, all our other fears have developed. And it remains there in the clearing, no matter how the world progresses. Daniel and Laura enter the house—and the narrative cuts off where we wake up from nightmares, so even our darkest dreams can't tell us what happened to Daniel and Laura next.

Follow You Home
A Sidekick to the Mark Edwards Novel

Part Two: London, November 2013, Chapters 9–15

It's been three months, and Daniel and Laura are transformed. The loss of identity that began with their stolen passports is complete. They are physically changed: paler, thinner, and ill-looking. Neither can function in their old life, neither at work nor in their relationship. Their one good night of feeling like they did before is ruined the next morning when they argue, and both accuse the other of not being themselves.

The Romanian police officer who interviewed them asked, "You have no identity?" He could have been referring only to their passports, but he seemed to recognize the house in the forest; he may have known what it did to them.

They can't forget or move on because even in England, they haven't escaped. They both constantly see death and horror around them. PTSD tells your brain that danger is ever-present; for Daniel and Laura, that might in fact be true. The robbery, Laura's near-death experience, and the man following her all suggest that what happened in Romania isn't over—but these events are also only witnessed by Daniel or Laura. What is apparition, and what is reality?

Follow You Home
A Sidekick to the Mark Edwards Novel

Daniel's insomnia and Laura's sleepwalking suggest that the divide between the conscious and unconscious, between reality and nightmare, is no longer simple for them.

Nor can they rely on anyone else's perception, as neither have any desire to share what happened. They are isolated by their secret, lost together in the dark long after they escaped the woods. Daniel's therapist pries, but the value of him re-exposing himself to the memories is unclear if danger is actually still present. His silence could be his survival.

Follow You Home
A Sidekick to the Mark Edwards Novel

Part Two: London, November 2013, Chapters 16–24

"And besides, if I bought a trap I'd probably walk into it myself."

Daniel no longer trusts himself. His forgetfulness, likely induced by alcohol and trauma, creates ominous "black spaces" in his mind, as though the darkness of Romania is now within him. Did someone else steal his debit card and overdraft his account, or did he? He buys a CCTV system, an impartial machine to filter reality for him, because he's so enmeshed in his own fear that he can't tell if he's seeing a pattern or if what he thinks he sees is just a projection of his mind.

Comelia becomes an embodiment of Daniel's paranoia and self-doubt. He reacts to her nationality and then tells himself it's nothing. She assures him that she's "not a vampire," but his subconscious recreates her in his dreams as a monster after his blood and stories. Her dropped phone is ominous: Alina and Laura lost their phones shortly before they entered the woods.

Unlike Laura, who is visited by a ghost and doesn't hesitate to believe it, Daniel is still clinging to the idea that his life should follow some inherent logic—and if it doesn't, then he must be crazy. Laura embraces the irrational, and unlike Daniel, she isn't tormented by the question of her sanity.

Jake in this section echoes the pleased, relaxed Daniel before Romania who had just sold his app. Jake has earned his success, Daniel says, like he did. "Barring a severe dose of bad luck," he says of Jake, "he was going to be a star." Daniel should know how powerful luck is, and how uncertain success is—but then, he still believes the world should make sense.

Follow You Home
A Sidekick to the Mark Edwards Novel

Part Two: London, November 2013, Chapters 25–33

In the snippet of story we get before being interrupted, we see Daniel struggling with the fundamental issue that still plagues him in the present: his superego attempting to conquer with logic the baser instinct to run. His gut tells him there must be a monster, but he tries to convince himself there is not. But Jake's sudden death, like Dr. Sauvage's—and like Laura disappearing into the snow without a trace—keeps him off-balance and out of control. He is never able to exorcise the fear that creeps through his every thought.

With video evidence on his side, though, Daniel's paranoia is turned outward. He creates a vast conspiracy to explain the tragedies in his life, with Comelia at the center. This kind of thinking allows for the possibility of returning to his good life, if he only uncovers and dismantles the conspiracy. This fight gives him a way to psychologically survive his current situation, and a fight against people is more winnable than one against insanity or amorphous evil.

The police, usually representatives of order and safety, do nothing to protect or aid Daniel. He is shunted from mainstream society because his problems are beyond comprehension. Edward, a private detective, also works on the fringes of society. That Edward survives the Molotov cocktail attack, another unpredictable moment in Daniel's life, is a commendation of Edward's ability to help him sort fact from paranoia at last.

Meanwhile, Laura is rapidly disengaging with ordinary life altogether. She quit her job and is spaced out and seeing ghosts everywhere. Even Erin's labor barely shakes her out of her otherworldly reverie. She won't try to kill herself, but can she live?

Part Three: Romania, August 2013 & Part Four: London, November 2013, Chapters 34–41

ALERT: SPOILERS BELOW

We have waited so long to hear this story; to finally get it is equal parts satisfying and dread-inducing. Daniel and Laura's behavior is understandable now: they didn't only witness the monstrosity in the house, they were also forced to participate in the crimes. In a violent and intense situation, they discover a side of themselves that they don't especially like.

Laura is preoccupied with the word *putrescent*. She ascribes it to herself, suggesting that part of her has died and is rotting, and that she continues to live after this death of who she once was. The rot is the part of herself she hates, her guilt for not saving Alina and the child. She also confuses "putrescent" with "pregnant": both processes involve a new growth inside the body that consumes it. And no wonder that birth and death are horribly intertwined for her—after visiting the house where babies are born and their mothers die.

Whether or not either of them recognizes it consciously, Daniel's choice to sacrifice the baby was the beginning of the end for their relationship. On some level, Laura must have wondered if she could have a child with him after he failed to protect the baby. Having children was a point of tension for them from the very beginning, and it became their breaking point after Romania.

Laura's encounter with Camelia and Daniel's realization of her motives are less satisfying. The plot of the drug dealers seems so banal compared to the horrors that Laura and Daniel beheld in the house. The reveal, coming from trustworthy Edward, that Alina is alive promises more mysteries—and as the prevalence of ghosts and phantoms suggests, death is not necessarily the end.

Could Daniel and Laura have saved the baby? Are they at all responsible for the deaths in the house?

Follow You Home
A Sidekick to the Mark Edwards Novel

Part Five, Romania, August-November 2013, Chapters 42–49

"All angels are terrifying."

Like Daniel and Laura, Alina and Ion had their own plans that were upturned when the border guards got hostile. And their lot, as they point out, is rougher than Daniel and Laura's, and the consequences of their choices harsher. If the plan had gone smoothly, Daniel and Laura would have been inconvenienced, but Ion, Alina, and Camelia's lives would have changed. Alina's description of them is indicative of this: "privileged without realising it, soft and gullible." Daniel and Laura are cushioned from certain realities that the Romanians are not, even as their lives get as bad as they ever have been—they couldn't even imagine the fate Alina suffered.

Alina's graphic novel is about rising up after death and finding justice. She, like Laura, goes through the motions of suicide only to return with a mission. She is born again, transformed by trauma. She rises from her coffin, the wooden room in which she had been left to die, then reclaims the identity that had been stolen from her by putting her own clothes back on. Murdering her captor is her first act, but his death is revenge, not justice—and it does not appease the restless souls of the twelve women who came before Alina.

One of the most frightening reveals of the chapter is that the man in the woods is not working alone—he is aided and abetted by some larger organization and with the approval of at least one policeman. The police in this novel range from unhelpful at best to truly evil, suggesting that justice can only be found by diverging from mainstream society, like Mirela does.

Follow You Home
A Sidekick to the Mark Edwards Novel

Part Six, London, November 2013, Chapters 50–56

Over the past months, Laura has been wracked with guilt about the baby she did not save. That guilt ruined her relationship with Daniel, led her to quit her job (where she was "letting down" other children), and eventually drove her to attempt suicide. The people who don't know the story of what happened in the house believe she might hurt little Oscar. In the back seat of the devil's car, though, Laura finally has a chance to redeem herself.

Daniel, too, sees his opportunity for redemption. Though Edward tells him not to blame himself, that he "didn't invite this chaos," he still takes responsibility for it, tracing it back to buying cheap tickets for the overnight train. Buying these tickets should not have been a fatal error, but he understands now how far-reaching the consequences of every decision can be. He also admits that Ion can make amends, recognizing on some level that Ion, like him, could not have predicted how terrible the situation would become.

The baby disappears while Erin and Rob are asleep; in fact, Oscar is sleeping when the old man kidnaps him. Sleep is a vulnerability. The mind becomes open to nightmares—Oscar going missing is truly Rob and Erin's worst nightmare, and Daniel and Laura's journey began when they fell asleep on the train. And yet people need sleep. It's an unavoidable part of life, which means no one is safe from nightmares, or the world changing around them while they slumber.

Follow You Home
A Sidekick to the Mark Edwards Novel

Part Six, London, November 2013, Chapters 57–62

In the climactic sequence, Laura and Daniel are both given a chance to redo what happened in the woods, and this time they are able to rescue Alina and the baby. The house in England is nearly identical to the one in Romania, as the fears it represents are universal rather than specific.

Laura and Daniel realize that what humans are capable of can be even worse than our nightmares of the paranormal. Gabor is not the devil or a phantom, Laura recognizes, "he was just a man." The benefit of believing in supernatural entities is that it puts evil at a safe distance from humanity; it is unbearable to imagine that a human could do to others what Gabor did. It's easier to live with the idea of witches and demons than acknowledge that people can do terrible things, and perhaps that the potential to be evil is within all of us. As Daniel points out, however, Gabor is "just a man. And men could be hurt." If evil is paranormal, then it is out of human control—but since Gabor is human, he can be stopped by human means.

Alina and Laura's conversation is significant as they reconstruct in a meaningful way the traumas they both experienced. If they hadn't gone into that house,

Alina points out, Gabor's operation could have continued for years undetected. The two women change the narrative of their pain, granting them control over it. Laura asks Alina if she's insane, and Alina responds, "Yes. We both are, aren't we?" Their "insanity" is not a negative quality, but a survival mechanism they developed in reaction to an irrational environment.

Follow You Home
A Sidekick to the Mark Edwards Novel

Part Seven, London, January 2014, Chapters 63–64 and Epilogue

The last two chapters give us a rosy portrait of Daniel and Laura's reunion. There is fallout from their adventure, their friendship with Erin and Rob a bit delicate, but Daniel seems committed to being optimistic. He suppresses his grief about Jake, apparently unwilling to let his thoughts be anything but positive. Edwards goes through all the motions of giving the couple a happy ending, but the sweetness of Daniel's chapters are cut by Laura's bitter epilogue.

The final missing piece of the story falls into place. Daniel was able to exploit our stereotyped expectations that women are the "natural" protectors of children and men are more selfish. Laura's extreme guilt and self-hatred drove her away from Daniel; she couldn't bear that he knew what she had done. And worse, she was compelled to protect her self-image by killing Jake, as if she could erase what she had done if no one knew about it. The potential for violence is within all of us if put under extreme pressure. Luckily for her, her plan to never confess complements Daniel's near-blind commitment to their relationship working out. For both of them, their identities depend on being together, no matter what.

Follow You Home
A Sidekick to the Mark Edwards Novel

Character Guide

Daniel Sullivan – a British app designer on vacation

Laura Mackenzie – Daniel's girlfriend; works for a children's charity

Ion and Alina – the Romanian couple on the train

Constantin – the police officer in Breva

Jake – Daniel's rock star best friend

Erin and Rob – Daniel and Laura's friends; expecting their first child

Dr. Claudia Sauvage – Daniel's therapist

Follow You Home
A Sidekick to the Mark Edwards Novel

Camelia – the Romanian woman at Jake's concert

Frank and Sandra – Laura's parents

Edward Rooney – a private detective

Sophie Carpenter – Rooney's assistant

Nicolae Gabor – a Romanian entrepreneur

Dragos – Gabor's son

Follow You Home
A Sidekick to the Mark Edwards Novel

A Closer Look:

Laura

We first see Laura from Daniel's perspective—he loves her dearly and sees only her best qualities. She is introduced to us as beautiful and kind: she does, after all, work for a children's charity. She makes an effort to connect with Alina, who also comes to like her. The biggest clue we get to her character in the first section of the book, however, is when Daniel mentions that she has a "dislike of breaking rules." She cares very much about how she appears to others, and she wants to be a good citizen. This desire to *look* like a good person leads Laura to make some of her worst mistakes throughout the story.

After they escape the Romanian house of horrors, Laura begs Daniel not to go to the police because she doesn't want anyone to find out what she had done, leaving Alina to be assaulted and the baby sold. She then kills Jake when she believes that he knows what happened. She is violently externalizing her self-hatred, attempting to erase the event by erasing knowledge of it. It also seems that her identity is very closely entwined with what others think of her—she seems to feel that in order to keep her shame hidden, she must kill. Her self-worth and self-esteem could be low as a result of growing up with critical and appearance-obsessed parents. Her successful self-presentation as a "good person" protects her from such criticism.

When everything starts to go wrong and her self-hatred is at an all-time high, Laura turns inward. She says that the experience in Romania ripped away the shell around her heart. Because she can no longer interact with the outside world, she gets lost inside her own mind. Her defense mechanism is to disengage: she quits her job, drifts away from her friends, and creates a fantasy world of ghosts and demons to compensate. She is able to come back to the real world once the danger has passed, but, as evidenced by her seeing the "crack" on the train, her mental state is still fragile.

Follow You Home
A Sidekick to the Mark Edwards Novel

Daniel

When Daniel first meets Camelia, she makes reference to Daniel in the lion's den: a Biblical story in which a righteous man is unfairly sentenced to death by lions. He is kept safe by God because he is blameless. Our Daniel is thrown into his own sort of lion's den, and he has to keep faith in himself to survive.

Daniel is a somewhat of a paradox. He's confident and proactive through most of the narrative: designing and selling his app, trying to save the baby from Dragos, and solving the mystery of the attacks on him and Laura. Even in his darkest time during the months following their return from Romania, he has the wherewithal to get a therapist in an attempt to regain control over his life. Still, he's very emotionally dependent on Laura. As Dr. Sauvage says to him when she asks him about himself, "You quickly start telling me about your girlfriend." Daniel retorts that his life is unremarkable. Laura's purpose, on a subconscious level, must be to elevate him above the unremarkable by the power of their true love. Perhaps this is why he is so committed to them reuniting: if he doesn't have her and their love story, then his life is without interest. The fact that Laura is somewhat unusual—her paranormal beliefs approaching psychosis in their intensity—makes her, and him by extension, even more interesting. He describes his relationship with Jake in a similar way: Jake, the cool musician who dragged him out of his own head.

Further, Daniel never expresses any sort of judgment toward Laura, despite knowing everything that she did in Romania. She needs someone who will love her unconditionally, which he does, and he needs someone to keep him on his toes—which she certainly will.

Follow You Home
A Sidekick to the Mark Edwards Novel

The Unreliable Narrator

The reveal that Daniel had changed the story of the house when he told it to Edward cements what we may have already suspected about him: that consciously or unconsciously he is not necessarily telling us the truth. First identified by literary critic Wayne C. Booth, the unreliable narrator misrepresents, intentionally or due to faulty perception, some fundamental elements of the story.

Laura is almost immediately recognizable as an unreliable narrator, as her trauma has clearly affected her perception of the world around her. Her belief in ghosts, also, is a sign that she sees the world in a markedly different way than the rest of us. Daniel, however, we trust. Even though he's been diagnosed with PTSD, he seems to be able to separate his hallucinations and flashbacks from reality—the paranoia, however, creeps in more insidiously. Even after learning that the fire at Dr. Sauvage's house was an accident, he keeps trying to blame people for it. When Alina confesses to Jake's murder, he automatically blames her for Claudia's death as well without a shred of evidence.

His misrepresentation of the story of the house, however, is intentional. We had no reason to believe he would lie to Edward, so we accepted it—but we didn't take into stock his biggest motivation throughout the story: his love of Laura. When we find out the truth in the epilogue, the lie is both shocking and understandable from a character perspective—the perfect twist.

Follow You Home
A Sidekick to the Mark Edwards Novel

Imagining Alternate Endings

What if Daniel and Laura had gone to the international police?

If Daniel was able to convince Laura to go to InterPol, it may have been difficult to get someone to investigate the house in the woods—but Alina and Luka may have been recovered before long. It's unlikely that Gabor would have been caught alongside his son, the grotesque Dragos, so he would have been out for revenge against Daniel and Laura.

Violence would be sure to follow, and without Alina to identify him as colluding with her captor, it would be more difficult to stop him.

Their backpacks with the cocaine would still have been abandoned, which means Camelia would have gotten involved in an attempt to recover them. Daniel and Laura's relationship, although at first under strain about telling the story, would have been stronger once it became clear that they saved Alina and the baby. Laura would be able to move past what she did in the house over time. Alina may have been able to capitalize on the extensive news coverage of her kidnapping and publish a tell-all graphic novel about her experience.

What if Edward Rooney had been killed in the attack on his office?

With yet another avenue for help destroyed, and no rational mind on his team to help him sort through the evidence, Daniel would have gone into a tailspin. His drinking would have become out of control, as would his paranoia. He would have concocted some grand conspiracy theory that would explain the deaths of Dr. Sauvage, Jake, and Edward in a way that wouldn't make sense to anyone else. The theory would have been centered around Camelia as the source of all his problems, so he would spend his time alternately trying to track her down and hanging around Erin and Rob's house to get Laura back—and he would eventually run into Alina, discovering that she's alive.

Both under duress, Alina and Daniel would pool their information and realize that there was another player in the game, the one who firebombed Rooney's office—Gabor. Of course, they wouldn't have the contact in the Breva police department, so they wouldn't know much about him, but they would know enough to be able to lure him into a trap with Alina as the bait.

Laura, however, would never fully recover from what happened in Romania without having had the chance to redeem herself by saving Oscar, although her friendship with Erin and Rob would still be strong.

Follow You Home
A Sidekick to the Mark Edwards Novel

Themes & Symbols You May Have Missed

Vampirism

The most famous vampire, Dracula, comes from Transylvania, an area in central Romania; he was based on the real and vicious Romanian general, Vlad the Impaler. In Romania, vampires are known as *strigoi*, and they have been associated with the area in popular culture ever since the release of Bram Stoker's novel. Daniel and Laura, two healthy adults, visit Romania, enter its woods—and return home pale, weak, and cold. Daniel drinks red wine constantly throughout the first half of the novel, and explicitly describes it as blood several times. Laura bites her nails until they bleed and then sucks the blood. Their transformation in the story is due to trauma, but can be read symbolically as vampiric.

These hints of vampirism not only add a creepy ambiance to the story, but they give us an interesting way to conceptualize Daniel and Laura's trauma. The comparison to life and death shows how deeply their experience in Romania affected them. They died in Romania on some level; they are now fundamentally different, and yet the same.

Vampirism also suggests the possibility of rising from the grave. Alina is assumed dead throughout most of the novel and has two presumed deaths: once when Daniel and Laura hear the gunshot and once again after faking suicide in order to kill her captor. "Blood, blood, glorious blood," she chants during the latter experience, because, though blood can be a harbinger of death, it is also a crucial component of life. She "dies" and then is born again, baptized by blood. Alina is unique in that she is tremendously motivated to stay alive and avenge the lives of the other women that Gabor killed. Her soul will not rest, so she survives these "deaths."

Gabor and his monstrous son are also vampires of a kind. They profit off of human suffering, "feeding" on their souls and bodies. Both Gabor and his predatory business also survive several deaths: Gabor is presumed dead after the end of the Communist era; the house in Romania is abandoned, only to rise again almost identically in England. Both of them only die under violent attack, again marked by a great deal of blood.

Photographs

Photographs float through this novel, voices of the past. Daniel has an expensive camera with which he documents his and Laura's luxurious vacation; he has invested in wanting to preserve their trip in some way. Unfortunately for Daniel and Laura, cameras are equally good at documenting the horrible. They are machines, unbiased and uncaring of what they record. The women and children who passed through Gabor's house of horrors are forever memorialized on the wall there in the form of photographs. Long after they are gone, the photographs remain as a marker, and likely a trophy, for Gabor and Dragos.

Many people throughout this novel want to forget what happened in their past or hide their past from the people around them. The presence of photographs emphasizes that this is impossible and that what has happened in our past cannot be erased. For better or worse, these events exist outside our heads. Daniel describes his memories of the house returning to him, "as if revealed by a camera flashing in the dark." Later, he goes through his vacation photographs, trying to remember how wonderful their trip had been, but he is surprised by two photos of him and Laura sleeping on the train. Those two photographs pop up to demonstrate that Daniel cannot undo what happened to him and Laura; he can't go back in time to before Romania.

Cameras, though, being impartial, are also used by Daniel to find his enemies. First, his video camera proves to him that he hasn't been imagining his persecution and gives him some evidence of who might be after him. The video of the dog sniffing leads Daniel to the revelation that Camelia is looking for drugs. Also, they discover Gabor's identity and connection to the rest of the case because of a photograph they find of him as a young Communist police officer.

Follow You Home
A Sidekick to the Mark Edwards Novel

Possible Storylines for a Prequel

Beatrice, the ghost from Laura's childhood, is one of the biggest unanswered questions left at the end of *Follow You Home*. The book doesn't fall one way or the other about the possibility of ghosts, and while strong hints are given that Laura has mental health issues, nothing is definitive. It would be interesting to see how Laura became the person that we see in *Follow You Home*, and the brief glimpse we get of her parents promises they could be interesting and complex characters in their own right.

Why, for example, did Laura's parents decide to put Laura in the strict all-girls school? What did Laura experience there? She became a very different person from her parents, working for a children's charity rather than trying to accumulate wealth, and this was likely a pivotal and decisive moment in her upbringing. It's possible that she did once have a good relationship with her parents and then something happened to distance her from them, likely during this tumultuous period. Maybe she started acting out beyond seeing ghosts; she could have started sneaking out to see her best friend, the one her parents thought was "too common."

It would be interesting to see what Beatrice was like and how her relationship with Laura developed. Laura seems to have had a lifelong affection for her, as well as believing in ghosts into adulthood because of her. Also, the violent circumstances that surrounded Beatrice's life and death could lead young Laura into a kind of cold case investigation. Her killer could still be at large and would not like a little girl asking a lot of questions and sticking her nose into the mystery. Whether Laura was mentally unstable, had an overactive imagination, or if Beatrice was real, would be a central tension throughout this prequel.

Follow You Home
A Sidekick to the Mark Edwards Novel

Hidden Clues

The man watching Laura in the park and the old man on the train were both Gabor. Was he creeping around anywhere else?

- "An old man had been spotted hanging around the maternity unit, hovering around the sick babies who were kept apart from their mothers. When staff challenged him, he strode off." This is almost certainly Gabor keeping an eye on Laura and either trying to kidnap a sick baby or just fantasizing about it. The other major clue is that he isn't cowed by the staff challenging him; he strides off, full of the confidence of a powerful and dangerous man.

- "A man I assumed to be Edward Rooney was seeing another man out of the office. Another client, I guessed, one with white hair, though I could only see his back." Presumably, Daniel made his appointment with Rooney over email on his hacked computer, which means that Gabor would have been able to make an appointment around the same time. He confirms that Daniel has arrived to meet with Rooney, and then has just enough time to disguise himself and prepare the Molotov cocktail before returning for the attack.

And how did Daniel not notice Laura being kidnapped right in front of his house? Laura recounts that Camelia comes screeching up in her silver car and then threatens her with a knife to get her into the car. Meanwhile, in the previous chapter, Daniel is upstairs working with Rooney: "At one point, I heard the sound of tyres skidding on the road outside, the thump of a car door. But I was concentrating too hard on what I was doing to look out of the window." If he had, he likely would have seen Camelia waylaying Laura.

Follow You Home
A Sidekick to the Mark Edwards Novel

In the Final Analysis . . .

Follow You Home transforms over the reading. At first, it's a story of a vacation gone wrong, of strangers in a strange land. It becomes a narrative about living with trauma and mistrusting your own mind. And it concludes as an investigation of the human capacity for evil. Our darkest fears come not from dark woods, but from what our fellow man may be doing there. But the novel isn't completely hopeless: though evil can't be undone, it can be stopped. Edwards seems to have most of his faith in the individual to fight back against wrongdoing—rather than social institutions like police or government. Daniel and Laura manage to dismantle Gabor's operation, though that doesn't mean these events will no longer affect them. The past can't be willed away, so they must find a way to live with it.

Could Daniel and Laura's relationship survive if Laura confesses, or would deception be kinder?

Follow You Home
A Sidekick to the Mark Edwards Novel

If You Loved This Novel . . .

The Magpies, Mark Edwards

Another psychological thriller by Edwards, his first, about an optimistic couple ready to settle down and have a family. In this novel, the horrors start not in a foreign country but at home, when they move into a new building. *The Magpies* is more claustrophobic than the continent-stretching mysteries of *Follow You Home*, but just as tautly suspenseful.

Mind of Winter, Laura Kasischke

The protagonist of *Mind of Winter* is Holly, a poet and a mother to an adopted daughter, Tatiana, who she and her husband brought home from a Siberian orphanage. The narrative is more lyrical and stream-of-consciousness than *Follow You Home*, and the plot less action-packed, but the suspense is still ramped up to unbearable levels as Holly and Tatiana are snowed into their house alone on Christmas Day. You will not be able to stop reading this book.

People Who Eat Darkness: The Fate of Lucie Blackman, Richard Lloyd Parry

A horrifying nonfiction account of a British girl who went missing abroad, *People Who Eat Darkness* is not a book you should read before visiting Japan. Parry does an exquisite job of cataloging every step of the investigation, media coverage, and cultural tensions as Lucie Blackman's family searches for her in the seedy underbelly of Tokyo.

So, What'd You Think?

Thanks for investing in this *Sidekick*. Now that you've read it, let us hear from you!

Follow You Home
A Sidekick to the Mark Edwards Novel

In just a sentence or two, please email founders@welovenovels.com your answer to one simple question:

What was your favorite (or least favorite) thing about this Sidekick?

We want to know what you think, so we can bring you more of what you love most, and fix what you don't like.

And if you would like a free copy of Katherine Miller's top-rated *Sidekick* to *Leaving Time,* Jodi Picoult's latest bestseller, we'd like to send it to you (a $4.99 value). All you have to do is add the words **"Yes, I Want My Bonus Sidekick"** to the email subject line, and you'll get instant access.

Follow You Home
A Sidekick to the Mark Edwards Novel

About the Author of This Sidekick

Elizabeth Halprin has been a hoarder of books from a young age, and the invention of the ebook has enabled her to continue this practice without the clutter. She lives in Boston with a weird little dog.

Follow You Home
A Sidekick to the Mark Edwards Novel

Other Sidekicks from WeLoveNovels

Sidekick to Go Set a Watchman

Sidekick to The Martian

Sidekick to Luckiest Girl Alive

Sidekick to Seveneves

Sidekick to All the Light We Cannot See

Sidekick to The Nightingale

Sidekick to Wayward

Sidekick to Seveneves

Sidekick to Departure

Sidekick to Orphan Train

Sidekick to Papertowns

Sidekick to Gathering Prey

Sidekick to Pines

Sidekick to Memory Man

Sidekick to The Shadows

Follow You Home
A Sidekick to the Mark Edwards Novel

Sidekick to The Husband's Secret

Sidekick to A Spool of Blue Thread

Sidekick to The DUFF

Sidekick to Insurgent

Sidekick to Redeployment

Sidekick to The Girl on the Train

Sidekick to Still Alice

Sidekick to Captivated by You

Sidekick to Catching Fire

Sidekick to Mockingjay

Sidekick to Deadline

Sidekick to Big Little Lies

Sidekick to Gone Girl

We are so grateful to all who have taken a moment to leave a quick review of one of our Sidekicks on Amazon. Your thoughtfulness means a lot and helps us, and the rest of the world, know how we are doing and how we can improve. :)

Follow You Home
A Sidekick to the Mark Edwards Novel

Questions? Ideas? Comments?

Email **founders@welovenovels.com**.

We are listening!

Follow You Home
A Sidekick to the Mark Edwards Novel

Copyright © 2015 by WeLoveNovels. All rights reserved worldwide. No part of this publication may be reproduced or transmitted in any form without the prior written consent of the publisher.

Limit of Liability/Disclaimer of Warranty: The publisher and the author make no representations or warranties with respect to the accuracy or completeness of the contents of this work and specifically disclaim all warranties, including without limitation warranties of fitness for a particular purpose. No warranty may be created or extended by sales or promotional materials. The advice and strategies contained herein may not be suitable for every situation. This work is sold with the understanding that the publisher is not engaged in rendering legal, accounting, or other professional services. If professional assistance is required, the services of a competent professional person should be sought. Neither the publisher nor the author shall be liable for damages arising herefrom. The fact that an organization or website referred to in this work as a citation and/or a potential source of further information does not mean that the author or the publisher endorses the information the organization or website may provide or recommendations it may make. Further, readers should be aware that the internet websites listed in this work may have changed or disappeared between when this work was written and when it is read.

Follow You Home
A Sidekick to the Mark Edwards Novel

Printed in Dunstable, United Kingdom